The Big Hairy Monster

Written by Seon-hye Jang
Illustrated by Min-oh Choi
Edited by Joy Cowley

One big hairy monster
lived in the deep woods.
Long hair covered his eyes
and because he looked scary,
the animals were afraid of him.
The monster had no friends.

Fall came to the woods.
The leaves changed color,
and the air grew cooler.

The big hairy monster
was all by himself.

One hairy monster! **1**

When winter brought snow,
everything was frozen.
The animals could not see
the big hairy monster.
They thought he'd gone away.

Two bears! 2

On a very cold day,
two shivering bears
found a cave in a heap of snow.
"Let's stay here and get warm."

Three wild boars! 3

Three wild boars,
snorting with the cold air,
found space under the snow.
"Let's stay here and get warm."

Four deer! 4

Four frozen deer,
tired of snow and ice,
found a place of shelter
in a great mound of snow.
"Let's stay here and get warm."

Five foxes! 5

Five furry foxes,
their hair stiff with ice,
found a hollow in the snow.
"We will be warm here."

Six raccoons! 6

Six raccoons with dripping noses
found a little valley in a mound of snow.
"This is where we'll be warm."

Seven pheasants! 7

Seven pheasants with cold tails
found a cozy nest in the snow.
"Let's stay here and keep warm."

Eight rabbits! 8

Eight rabbits, ears red with cold,
found a small burrow in the snow.
"We will be warm here."

Nine squirrels! 9

Nine squirrels with chattering teeth
found a hollow in a snowy hill.
"Let's stay here," they said.

Ten field mice! 10

Ten field mice, their tails stiff with ice,
found a hole in a valley of snow.
"Let's stay here and get warm."

Everyone found a way to stay cozy
that long, cold winter.
Time passed and days grew warm.
Finally, spring melted the snow.

Where was the big hairy monster during that long, cold winter?

The hairy monster wanted friends.
Now he had so many friends,
he couldn't count them.
Can you count them for him?

Where are the friends?

The big hairy monster found his friends.

Let's count them with him.

One bear on a rock **1**

Two wild boars on a log **2**

I found you!
I found you!

Three rabbits behind a mound **3**

Four deer in a field
4

Five squirrels in a tree
5

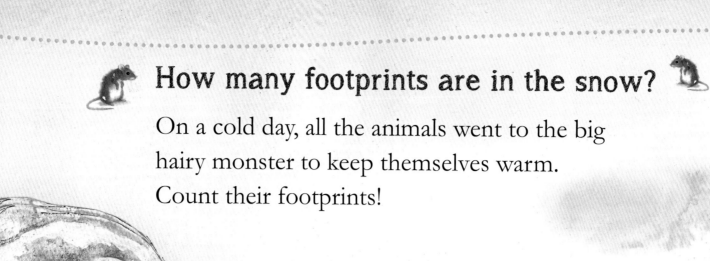

How many footprints are in the snow?

On a cold day, all the animals went to the big
hairy monster to keep themselves warm.
Count their footprints!

one, two, three, four, five, six!

6

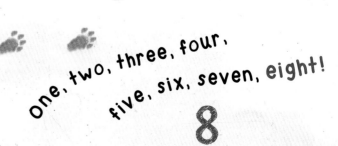

one, two, three, four,
five, six, seven, eight!

8

10

One, two, three, four, five, six, seven, eight, nine, ten!

One, two, three, four, five, six, seven!

7

One, two, three, four, five, six, seven, eight, nine!

9

Original Korean text by Seon-hye Jang

Illustrations by Min-oh Choi

Korean edition © Yeowon Media Co., Ltd.

This English edition published by big & SMALL in 2016
by arrangement with Yeowon Media Co., Ltd.
English text edited by Joy Cowley
English edition © big & SMALL 2016

Distributed in the United States and Canada by
Lerner Publishing Group, Inc.
241 First Avenue North
Minneapolis, MN 55401 U.S.A.
www.lernerbooks.com

ISBN: 978-1-925247-04-6

Printed in Korea